Dear Parents:

Congratulations! Your child is taking the first steps on an exciting journey. The destination? Independent reading!

STEP INTO READING® will help your child get there. The program offers five steps to reading success. Each step includes fun stories and colorful art or photographs. In addition to original fiction and books with favorite characters, there are Step into Reading Non-Fiction Readers, Phonics Readers and Boxed Sets, Sticker Readers, and Comic Readers—a complete literacy program with something to interest every child.

Learning to Read, Step by Step!

Ready to Read   Preschool–Kindergarten
• big type and easy words • rhyme and rhythm • picture clues
For children who know the alphabet and are eager to begin reading.

Reading with Help   Preschool–Grade 1
• basic vocabulary • short sentences • simple stories
For children who recognize familiar words and sound out new words with help.

Reading on Your Own   Grades 1–3
• engaging characters • easy-to-follow plots • popular topics
For children who are ready to read on their own.

Reading Paragraphs   Grades 2–3
• challenging vocabulary • short paragraphs • exciting stories
For newly independent readers who read simple sentences with confidence.

Ready for Chapters   Grades 2–4
• chapters • longer paragraphs • full-color art
For children who want to take the plunge into chapter books but still like colorful pictures.

STEP INTO READING® is designed to give every child a successful reading experience. The grade levels are only guides; children will progress through the steps at their own speed, developing confidence in their reading.

Remember, a lifetime love of reading starts with a single step!

For a wonderful dad,
Bob Miller —*J.L.*

Step into Reading, Random House, and the Random House colophon are registered trademarks of Penguin Random House LLC.

Visit us on the Web!
StepIntoReading.com
randomhousekids.com

Educators and librarians, for a variety of teaching tools, visit us at RHTeachersLibrarians.com

ISBN 978-0-7364-3755-4 (trade) — ISBN 978-0-7364-9022-1 (lib. bdg.)
ISBN 978-0-7364-3756-1 (ebook)

Printed in the United States of America   10 9 8 7 6 5 4 3 2 1

DISNEY PRINCESS

I Love My Dad

by Jennifer Liberts

illustrated by Francesco Legramandi
and Gabriella Matta

Random House 🏠 New York

Merida loves her dad.
He is silly!

King Fergus is strong.
He shows Merida
how to use a sword.

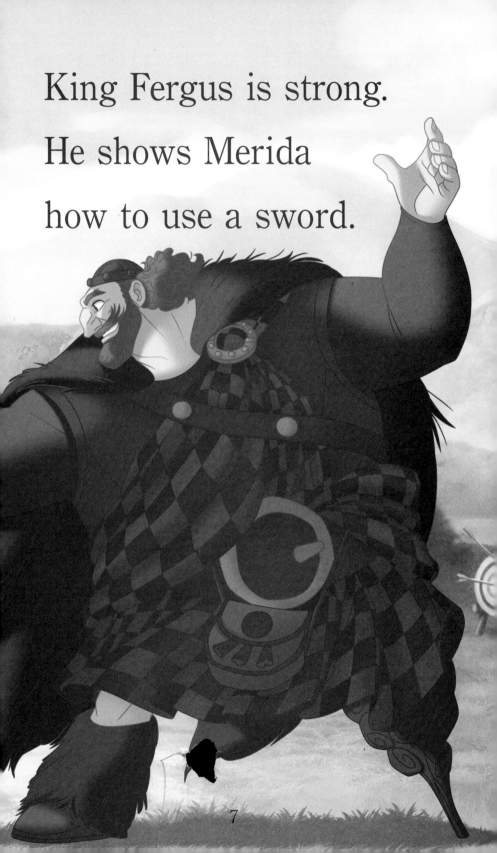

Rapunzel loves
her dad.
He is kind.

King Frederic
and Rapunzel take care
of their horses.

Rapunzel shows
King Frederic
how to paint.

Belle loves
her dad, Maurice.
He is smart.
They like
to invent together.

Belle shows her dad
her favorite book.

Ariel loves her dad.
King Triton is proud
of Ariel.
She sings for him.

King Triton teaches
Ariel about the sea.

Jasmine loves
her dad.
He is friendly.
They visit
the market together.

Jasmine and the Sultan
ride camels.
They like spending time
side by side.

The princesses
love their dads!